The Adventures of FOUR CREATIVE WIZ KIDS

All Aboard The Chocolate Bar

Frances Bildner

'Where to, Jess,' shouted Nick to his brother.
'We could cross the world from one side to the other.
Imagine the world as a Chocolate Biscuit
Come on Jess, shall we risk it?'

'Sure. We'd eat it from China to the U S of A.
Covered in chocolate, we'd run and play.
Tash and Gen can come along too,
Around the world with me and you.'

Jess and Gen climbed chocolate bars
Flying through space nearly at Mars

Whirling and circling the sun and the moon
Singing together - a happy tune

But then a Witch called out,
'I want all the coins you've got,
Or else you'll end up
in a big black pot

Full of snakes, worms
and sticky glue.
You think I'm joking,
the four of you?'

Nick said, 'Your threatening ways don't frighten us.
We're not here to make a fuss.
We're not giving a thing away.
We came in peace and just want to play.'

'Nick,' whispered Jess.
'Maybe we should run. I'm frightened.
This isn't any fun.'

The witch's red nails became a huge hook.
And in her fury she screamed and shook.
Nick said, 'We don't believe you have any magic.
All you have are your coins, that's actually quite tragic.'

The witch wrapped her hook hands around the broom
And spun madly around, vava voooom.
Grabbing Jess, Gen Tashie, not Nick
Cackling and hissing she flew really quick.

Nick said, 'Zap, Zoom,
Olla, Olla, Olla.
Got to get help from
my friend Walla.
The Witch with all
the coins in the east
Wants to make Jess
and my friends into a feast.'

Jess, Tash and Gen were locked in the castle of gold.
'Shine my coins!' screeched the witch. 'Do as you're told!'
Tash said to a rat, 'Nick will rescue us soon,
He'll be hatching a plan from his beach on the moon.'

'Enough,' said the Witch. 'For one afternoon.
I don't like your stupid tune.
Get back to work, there's shining to be done.
Do you really think this is a castle of fun?

The only thing in this world that I'm after,
The only thing which fills me with laughter,
Are my golden coins and lots more money.
Wiz kids, do you think I'm being funny?

Abracadabra and goobly goo,
I'm boiling up my witch snake stew.
You'll join the worms,
rats, snakes and slugs.
By the time I am finished
you'll end up as bugs"

Then Nick surfed in
on a chocolate wave.
Jess said, 'Surf rescue!
What a rave!

Walla, too on a huge
chocolate biscuit"
"Told you Jess
you gotta risk it!"

Walla said Mouth open wide.
'Come on, Witchie, come on inside.
You think you're so clever with your coins of gold,
But the truth is, Witchie, you're not very bold.'

THE END

This book is dedicated to My grandson Dillon
and my granddaughter Laila and to all
creative wiz kids in the world!